ERIC MADDERN studied sociology and psychology at Sheffield University, then spent 10 years travelling around the world. He now performs all over the country as a storyteller and folk singer at schools, colleges, galleries, forests, gardens, museums and festivals. He lives in western Snowdonia where he has created Cae Mabon, an eco-retreat centre which was, in 2008, declared the number one natural building project in the UK. Eric's other books for Frances Lincoln are *Death in a Nut*, *Nail Soup*, *Cow on the Roof*, *Earth Story* and *Life Story*, *The King with Horse's Ears*, *Spirit of the Forest*, *Rainbow Bird*, *The King and the Seed* and *Curious Clownfish*.

FRANÉ LESSAC is an internationally known American artist who has exhibited her paintings in London, Paris, New York and Los Angeles. From film school in California she went on to study Caribbean culture on the island of Monserrat. She has illustrated over 30 books for children. In 2010 she was awarded The Muriel Barwell Award for Distinguished Service to Children's Literature. Frané lives in Fremantle, Australia.

For respect and goodwill between the peoples of the Earth – E.M.

For Mark – F.L.

First published in Great Britain in 1993 by Frances Lincoln Children's Books
This edition published in Great Britain and in the USA in 2015
by Frances Lincoln Children's Books,
74–77 White Lion Street, London N1 9PF
www.franceslincoln.com

A catalogue record for this book is available from the British Library.

ISBN 978-1-84780-652-9

Printed in China

1 3 5 7 9 8 6 4 2

THE FIRE CHILDREN

A WEST AFRICAN FOLK TALE

Frances Lincoln
Children's Books

Long ago Nyame, the great sky-god, lived alone in the wide
blue sky. One day he took a basket and filled it with earth,
trees, flowers, insects and birds, and he hung it in the sky.
That basket was the Earth.

Then he made a round trapdoor in the sky so that he could
climb down to visit the Earth, with little holes so that the
light could shine through when the trapdoor was shut.
The trapdoor and holes were the moon and the stars.

One day Nyame was looking through his trapdoor moon admiring the Earth down below. But deep inside him two little spirit people were curious. They wanted to see what was going on.

So they climbed up Nyame's throat, into his mouth, over his tongue and were just looking through his teeth when he let out a tremendous sneeze.

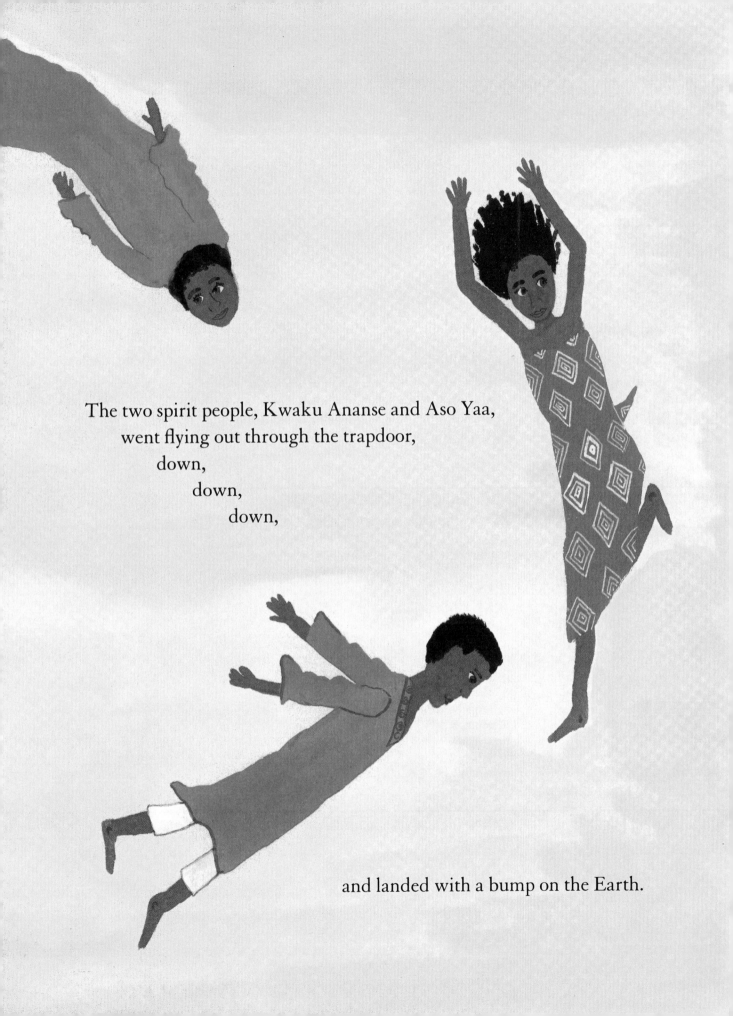

The two spirit people, Kwaku Ananse and Aso Yaa,
went flying out through the trapdoor,
down,
   down,
      down,

and landed with a bump on the Earth.

They picked themselves up and looked around at the tall trees and hanging vines, the dark pools and splashing streams, the brilliant birds flashing through the leaves. Nearby they found a warm cave and decided to make it their home.

Each day they went outside to explore, to sing with the wind and dance with the falling leaves.

One day Aso Yaa was lonely, and she stayed at home in the
cave. When Kwaku Ananse returned she had a big smile on
her face.

"Oh Aso Yaa of many moods," he said, "when I left this
morning you were sad. Now you are glowing like a hibiscus
flower. What is it?"

"I have an idea," she said.

"Not another idea!" said Kwaku Ananse. "Last time you
had an idea we were inside Nyame. Now look where we are!"

"Listen," said Aso Yaa. "It will not hurt you to listen."

"First we take some clay," Aso Yaa began,
"and mould it into little shapes just like us,
with arms and legs and heads. Then we bake
them in the fire and when they are cooked we
breathe life into them. We could call
them children."

"That's not a bad idea," said Kwaku
Ananse. So the next day Aso Yaa dug up clay
outside the cave and they made a hot glowing
fire. Then they shaped little figures like
themselves and put them on the fire to bake."

Suddenly, they heard crashing footsteps outside in the forest. Nyame had come to visit. Frightened that they were doing wrong, Kwaku Ananse and Aso Yaa snatched the little clay figures from the fire, wrapped them in leaves and hid them at the back of the cave.

Nyame's face appeared at the mouth of the cave.

"Well, my spirit people," he said, "are you enjoying my Earth?"

"Oh yes, Nyame," they replied.

"Are you being good?"

"Oh yes, Nyame," they answered, "we're being very good."

"Well, take good care of everything I have made," Nyame boomed, and then he disappeared.

Next day, Aso Yaa made a new batch of clay children, but no sooner had they begun to bake than Nyame was back again.

This time the spirit people had no time to take out the little figures. Instead, they stood in front of the fire hiding their work. And this time Nyame stayed talking for a long time. Maybe he suspected something. By the time he was gone, the clay children were baked quite black.

And so it went on. Every day they made more shapes and put them in the fire. And every day Nyame called to see them. Sometimes they heard him coming and were able to take the children out of the fire. Sometimes they had to leave them in the fire until he had gone.

But at last Nyame climbed back through the trapdoor moon and into the sky world above.

Then Kwaku Ananse and Aso Yaa spread out all the fire children. Some were hardly cooked at all and were white. Some were rosy pink, some honey yellow, some dusky red, some nut brown – and some midnight black. Kwaku Ananse and Aso Yaa loved them all, because they were their children.

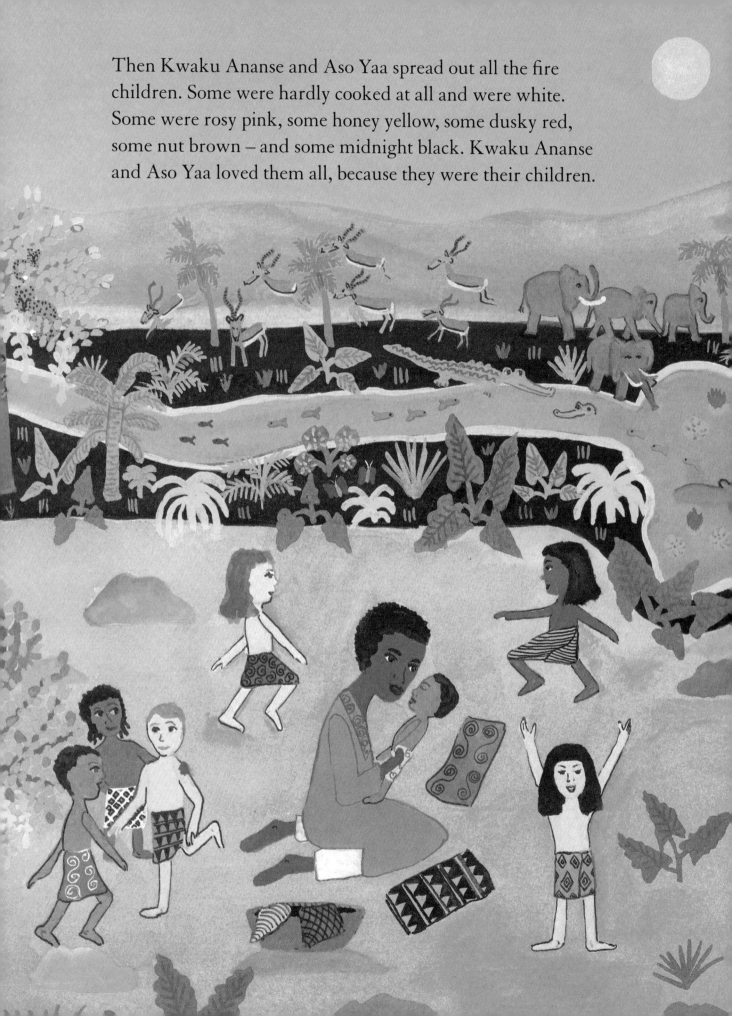

Now the spirit people breathed life into the fire children. One by one they awoke, yawned, stretched and opened their eyes, just like children waking up in the morning. Then they stood up and went off to play.

Years later, when the fire children
grew up, they wandered to all corners
of the Earth and had children of their own.
And their children had children.

And that is why today the Earth is
filled with people of many different
colours – black, white, red,
brown, yellow and pink.
Kwaku Ananse and Aso Yaa
love them still.

They always will.

MORE TITLES BY ERIC MADDERN
FROM FRANCES LINCOLN CHILDREN'S BOOKS

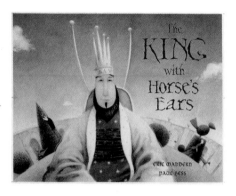

THE KING WITH HORSE'S EARS
Eric Maddern
Illustrated by Paul Hess

No-one knows about King Mark's ears except his barber. Keeping the secret eventually drives him to the doctor, who advises him to whisper it to the ground. But sooner or later, truth will out…

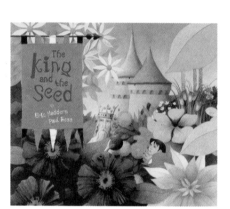

THE KING AND THE SEED
Eric Maddern
Illustrated by Paul Hess

Old King Karnak is worried. He hasn't long to live, and there is no heir to the throne. So he holds a rather unusual competition to find one. Knights and nobles flock to the palace and the King gives each of them a tiny seed to grow. Jack the farmer's son is given a seed too, so he plants it, waters it and waits for it to sprout…

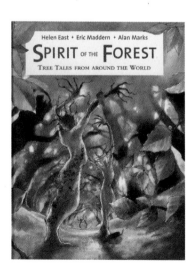

SPIRIT OF THE FOREST
Tree Tales from around the World
Helen East and Eric Maddern
Illustrated by Alan Marks

Trees are symbols of life itself. We cut them down at our peril. Here is a leafy anthology of 12 traditional tales from all over the Earth's surface from Native North America to New Guinea and from Wales to Nepal.

Frances Lincoln titles are available from all good bookshops.
You can also buy books and find out more about your favourite titles,
authors and illustrators on our website: www.franceslincoln.com